Heartbreak and Lust

reproduced, distributed or transmitted by any means without prior written consent from the author.

This book is dedicated to Chelsea and Chloe.
Without you both, I would have never powered through.

Trigger warnings:
Please be advised before reading this book explores themes of childhood trauma, self-harm, suicide, mental health related issues, and violence.

Chapters

HEARTBREAK

I still feel the thread connecting the two of us,
Pulling taught, memories flood my mind,
Sometimes I find myself thinking of you,
And I wonder why?
Wonder what you are doing,
Wonder if you think of me,
Wonder if it may have worked out in another reality.

We were lifetimes ago,
Vulnerable,
I hibernated,
Buried deep within me was my pain,
I thought you could take it all away.

Rebuild me from something new,
Forging strength together,
The electricity grew.

But you grew distant,
The story you wove became old,
Our spark had died,
I cut the thread, and still survived.

-It wouldn't surprise me if I heard from you again

I see little pieces of him in me,
I can pick up a pack of cigarettes so easily and I think about
school rides in his truck with him lighting up next to me,
When I get angry,
I can't breathe,
I want to scream and break things and then I think about
that bowl he threw at her feet and the crashes in the
bedroom on early mornings.
When life gets tough, I want to turn to anything that will
take it all away, but then I remember his time away from us
all getting clean again just to pick up another vice.
I try to remind myself I am good enough, but am I not good
enough to feel the love from my father?

-We loved each other once, but I don't think we will again

Salt looks like sugar,
It's easy to wear a disguise if you learn how,
Quiet, demure, thoughtful, kind and caring,
But your tongue doesn't taste the same.

Vodka and water are two very different liquids,
One is smooth down your throat and the other burns.
But in the right glass they're both the same.

So how can you trust anyone?
Even red riding hood believed her grandmother was the
wolf.

-Looks can be deceiving darling

I couldn't cry for months,
Staring at empty spaces,
Willing the dam to break,
For a reprieve of my feelings,
I dug myself a hole and let the soil cover me,
I couldn't breathe.
I planted a seed but couldn't water it to grow,
The season passed,
With nothing to harvest.

-Why can't I cry?

Lightly, fingers brush over piano keys,
The wrong chord struck twice,
Loud muttering rings through an empty living room where
living does not occur,
The sofa is sunken in on the sides from bodies that no
longer remain in this house,
Crumbs scattered onto the cream carpets that someone
previously lovingly looked after,
Wooden coffee table covered in coffee stains and water
rings,
The stale smell of cigarettes and sweat permeates the air,
A home that was proud to a house that ... just is.

-That house is gone now

Someone loved me once.
They loved me enough to keep me for years,
Sleep by my side every night,
They listened to me laugh and smiled back at me,
We watched rubbish telly on the weekends,
And had long walks by the sea.

We went for dinners out and stayed up talking all night.
One day it all changed, over half a decade had gone by,
Our vows to love each other meant nothing at all,
Those hand written notes kept in my underwear draw are
now ash in the wind,
The birthday cards I collected have been ripped up in
malice.

You threw it all away for a girl you barely knew,
7 years of us and all we went through,
I thought we could get *through*.

Offered you an out, a loop, a saving grace,
But you didn't want to save us,

-Did you?

-How many times must I live through heartbreak in my life?

We cooked together most nights before you left,
You always said "I'll buy you a sieve,"
We laughed about how stubborn I was,
Refusing adamantly to buy one,
You caught stray strands of spaghetti,
Burnt fingers and red hands,
"I'm buying you a sieve" you said the last time I saw you,
And somehow, I knew you never would.

-Will I ever be enough?

Blue eyes,
Not like the ocean on a summer's day,
Not like the sky when the sunshine is here to stay,
Not the type of blue that brings light in your heart,
Your blue eyes were like a stormy sea,
I was on a boat, pulled into your whirlpool,
The thunder and lightning sounded but I ignored their pleas,
I settled into my new home under water,
I made peace with my new enemies,
I grew a child out of our broken love,
Broken promises,
Broken trust and thriving lies,
Out she came into the world,
But just like you,
Blue eyes.

- I wish she had eyes like mine, but every time she looks at me, all I see is you

Can you long for what you have never had?
My chest feels like an empty cave of emotion waiting for
someone to fill it,
I cannot contain my organs anymore,
Someone please sew me up,
Every bite of food tastes like dry soil in my mouth,
Someone try to plant some seeds in me so my stomach
feels full,
I am growing something new in my belly,
Words are like stalks of a plant growing out from my jaws,
The leaves are taking over,
The plant has created spores.
I can't **fucking** take this anymore.

This tree or **THING** I have growing inside of me,
Its crushing my bones,
I am suffocating,
The bark from the tree is growing around me,
I can't feel the sunshine on my skin,
I cannot even begin,
I have no ending,
I am nothing.

-Alone

I wonder how the lies tasted on your tongue,
Where they thick and sweet like honey,
Clogging up your throat?
Did you taste remorse when you did it over and over?
Did the lies take up all the space in your brain, tripping
over them as they got bigger.
A snowball of lies causing an avalanche in your mind,
I wonder if anxiety stole air from your lungs every time I
saw her name pop up on your phone,
Every time you said "I love you" did you feel your stomach
drop into the core of the earth and burn.
When you kissed me goodnight, did your lip's taste sour
because they weren't hers?

-Why did you leave me? Why did you leave us? Why didn't
you say anything?

Back to black plays loudly on a second hand piano in a
smoke-filled room,

My voice doesn't reach through the walls of my bedroom as I sing along,
The melody reminds me of a time where my hips and waist were smaller and I lived off cigarettes and watermelon,
My hair cascaded down my back and my eyeliner thick and heavy,
Fingers always plucking the strings of an old guitar that was never mine,
The house was stocked with wine but not much else,
Transported, this was Amy Winehouses house.

-He always went back to black

Insecurities wind around my neck like a noose,
My mind whispers and mumbles to me, filling me with
doubt.

"I will never achieve my hopes and dreams,"
"No one will ever love me,"
"My situation won't improve,"
"This weight won't disappear,"
The words spiral around my mind,
I stand on the chair ready to kick it away from me until a
voice of reasons tells me to stop,
Red is all I see.

-I am glad that I didn't do it, but my heart is still completely
broken

You are not the first to leave,
The world forgot me.
The undiagnosed – diagnosed problem.
A girl all men want and all men eventually leave.
I serve myself up on a silver platter,
A chameleon who changes her skin to be your desires,
Please don't leave.

I have reinvented myself in fits of mania,
In the highs I plaster myself in hair dye,
Trowelling on makeup,
Confined in the box I put myself in,
"Not a good enough daughter"
"Not a good enough wife"
"Not a good enough mother"
Everyone leaves me,
Please don't leave.

My ribcage is made of titanium,
Heart and lungs imprisoned,
I can scarcely breath or allow myself to feel,
The sun does not touch my skin with its warmth.

-Please don't leave

Don't let go of my hand,
Please.
I am torn between my head and heart,
Methodically the cogs in my mind tick,
Over thinker.

I thought I was unfeeling and cold,
An unlovable soul,
Stone heart beating in a lead chest.

I knitted together threads of fate and wove them into a
basket,
They carry every scrap of humanity I have left,
Every time I reinvented myself to be something someone
else wanted,
It was written down and stored away.

Watch me burn and break,
Retaliate,
I will come back stronger than I have before,
My own salvation,
Each time I rise from the ashes,
A Phoenix.

-I am stronger now

Jaggedly he carved his name into my porcelain skin,
A puppet for him to play with,
He tied me up with strings,
Then he asked me to dance, so I danced.

A performer on a stage,
The spotlights heat is burning my skin,
I couldn't break a sweat with eyes always upon me,
He will pull my strings to make me twirl again.

A perfect marionette handmade for him,
Moulded carefully with precision,
Modest clothing covering a women's curves,
Hair cut short and sharp – all in his control.

Force fed "I'm sorry" and "I love you" for breakfast, lunch
and dinner,
No snacks between meals because he needs to watch my
figure,
He can sense if I think a thought for myself and reminds me
who owns me,
His little play thing.

-Ex's are ex's for a reason

We lived, but we were barely alive,
Animated corpses slowly decaying inside,
Souls shrivelling like dying flowers,
Words barely exchanged,
Our voice boxes disappeared,
But we still choked on lies we hid.

We let ourselves slowly die,
Running on a wheel of societal expectations,
I could have left and freed myself so many times,

Hands were held out to me to hold,
Escape plans made but never gone through with.

I could have lived,
But I let myself die with you.

-Can corpses feel pain?

A morgue held more life than you,
Toothless smiles,
Dead eyes,
How we continued is to my surprise,
Enough silence between us to fill a graveyard,
Dead flowers rot in the bottom of the bin,
My mind was awash with cardinal sin,
I must have been a necrophiliac,
Loving the undead and wishing for love to be returned,
But if a heart doesn't beat,
Does that mean it cannot love?

-I would love you dead or alive

The spark left his eyes,
I watched the flames dance for months,
Until one day they fizzled out and died,
Someone poured water onto the hearth,
He lit a new one for her,
His smiles lacked teeth,
Body turned away from me,
He had already left me then,
No more cups of tea in bed while whispering sweet
somethings,
I have sweet nothing,
Just a hole in my chest,
And my heart under your feet.

-I didn't want to miss you, but I did

I am,
Too much.

A hearty loud laugh which echos throughout the room,
Bright and loud,
I speak before I think,
I think after I speak,
Overthinking takes hold of my body like I am possessed.

I open my mouth and my words escape like butterflies out
of a box,
They fly too far for me to reach and stuff them back into
my mouth,
Wings fragile as the words I speak,
As colourful as the clothes that cover my unsightly figure,
Too beautiful for this world.

-I am entirely too much

You were a labour of love,
I bared the fruits,
Only choosing the ripest and juiciest- you threw the rest of
me way,
I was past my expiry,
Boring,
Dull and lifeless.

A tree without leaves,
A new orchard started to grow across the way,
You visited it almost every day,
Forgetting that trees have seasons,
I bloomed again.

- Its funny, when you left me, flowers began to grow

I hold up a candle to light my way through another blurry
November night,
Holding onto lingering hope that things may get better,
The sky draping dreams across this city,
While I sit and try to write into the late hours.

Sobs escape my chest,
Bone rattling noises from barely parted lips,
The ghost of you haunts this room,
Inherited anger threatening to spill with these tears,
Thoughts that leach out of me are an unwelcomed guest.

I long for connection of any kind,
A blank page greets me,
I could lie in the dark,
Waiting for sleep to take me,
But these bittersweet feelings will still wait for me when I
rise.

-The winter brings out the best and worst of us

He asked if I would call him home,
A derelict building with no life,
Old curtains hung from the windows,
Post piled outside the front door,
I picked up my toolbox and went inside for shelter.

Hot tears roll down my cheeks,
The remains of makeup rolling with it,
There is a difference to being alone and being lonely.
Alone is something you can choose to be,
I sit and write alone with candles lit,
I lay alone in the bath, enjoying the smell of lavender in the
air.

But I am most lonely when I wake up and see no one's head
on the pillow next to mine,
On Saturday nights I am lonely,
Watching TV alone until I cannot stand the ache in my
chest,
When it's just my daughter and I playing in the park,
And I see the families around me laughing and it's just her
and I,
I wonder if she's notices.

-Every time this happens my heart shatters a bit more

Addiction has made its home in my veins,
Always just my father's daughter,
A packet of cigarettes here,
We're sat down on a broken garden chair,
My thoughts are out for slaughter,
Lungs slowly turning black as the shadows in my soul,
The red wine makes me feel alive again.
What's a healthy coping mechanism when you pick up
vices like dimes,
Another doctor tells you that you should seek help for your
mental health,
But I have no mental health,
I've come here for some mental help,
The GP opens my mouth and pushes in pills because he's
being paid for it,
Making my cravings dig a bit deeper,
My emotions a little bit darker,
Time to dig a hole 6 feet deep and lie in it.

-The pills stopped working years ago

I lie awake tonight,
Wondering how time has gone by.
I am staring at golden curls on the pillow next to mine,
A tiny body curled up, soft breaths and twitching brows,
Beneath her fluttering eyelids are blue orbs that remind me
of a mediterranean sea,
I cradle my baby in my arms,
But she isn't a baby anymore,

She is a girl.

-Where does the time go?

The worst day of my heartbreak,
Was the day you forgot the colour of my eyes.
There just like mine, you said.
I gasped softly,
I knew your eyes as well as I knew my own,
Orbs of grey and blue like a stormy sea
The waves crashing in front of me.
But my eyes,
My eyes are the colour of grass before the winter,
Green like moss, with specs of brown like the colour of
autumn leaves.
I hope in time, I forget the stormy seas.
That I'll find a new pair of eyes staring at me.

- The worst day of my heartbreak

Back at square once again,
Collecting broken hearts like daisies for a chain,

Another man promised me the moon on a string,
Promises broken one to many times,
I've captured red flags all my life,
I know how to spot them now,
Or so I think.

I stand on that first square again,
Looking at the chess board with barely any pieces left to play with,
Black and white kings and queens waiting on the other side,
Will I play with just the knights,
Or am I simply stuck with the pawn.

-I haven't played chess lately

Is hell a consequence of our actions?
Will I meet you in the fiery depths?
I know my father will meet me there,
Open arms in the flames,
A one-armed embrace, his other hand clutches a bottle.
My friends call me kind and merciful but inside I am just a
rotten apple.
My core is as black as ash.
Forgiveness is a fragile gift not many give,
It is not a one-way ticket to Nivarana,
"Sorry" does not undo all your wrongdoings,
Will your hands regret holding the knife that stabbed me in
the back?

-This was hard to write

When I picked my bleeding heart up off the floor,
I stuffed it back in my chest,
It was so small,
I was afraid it wouldn't stay.
A tiny hand picked up mine and spoke
"Don't worry mummy, it will be alright."

She stuck a unicorn plaster on my chest,
Her arms around my neck, she patted my head.

-My daughter is the love of my life.

I think my tears would fill the bath,
I'd sink below the salty water,
I might forget to hold my breath,
Life is just breathing,
And breathing is for the living.

Sodium Chloride burns my eyes,
Mouth wide ready to scream silently,
But I cannot seem to shed a tear.

-Even watching Marley and me I didn't cry

I never liked affection in the way it was given to me,
So freely, but so confining,
It felt so constricting and tiring,
Grabbed in places I never liked,
My hand wasn't held, but my head was held high,
The kisses were wet and watery,
Watered down like father's whisky on a Friday night,
The passion withered and died like the last flowers I
received,
Always an afterthought.

His arms felt like home at first,
But then the house was on fire,
The light slowly died, the smoke remained,
A house burnt to ashes,
They all blew away.

- Home is where the heart is.

I guess, I should have known from the start,
Desperate calls, and unwanted texts,
I didn't want to be alone, so instead I was alone with you,
You never got on one knee, you never proclaimed your
profound love for me,
I never got birthday balloons or a homemade cake that was
burnt but made out of love,
I wrote you letters, made you scrap books,
I mended your socks and learnt your favourite meals,
Although everything I make tastes like dust,
It was just for you,
Evenings stuck inside my own mind,
A lonely place to be,
I allowed you to rule my world,
But I never was a priority in yours.

-I wouldn't change anything though

The first man who broke my heart was you dad.

You stopped showing up,
Stopped being present,
Your spot on the sofa grew cold,
Once upon a time you were my best friend,
My protector,
A little girls knight in shining armour.

When the nightmares started, I would find you,
"Daddy will make the bad guys disappear"
You would say,
But as I grew older,
The bad guys became real,
And you were far away.

So, I looked for parts of you I wanted in people that I met,
Allowed poor treatment just for anything I could get,
I accepted I was worth less,
The nightmares still continue,
Almost most nights,
And I have learnt how to deal with bad guys myself.

-My nightmares are much different these days

I am sick and tired of thoughts of you consuming me,

The space in my brain is so precious so why does your
name circle round like a wheel,
I am exhausted,
I wish I could erase your face,
Your name,
Your laugh,
Your moans,
The sound of your voice,
The smell of your skin,
Until you are just a ghost.

-I wish you would ghost me

The second to last finger on my left hand is empty,
The silver band I wore for many years discarded,
A play thing for my anxiety,
A symbol of forever,
A symbol of together,
Erased with good measure.

My hand feels naked,
Lonely,
Lost,
But not...

Wrong?

-I wore no rings on this finger before,
And perhaps I never will again.

Your heart can break in so many ways,
The first time it broke is when I realised my father had
given up,
I was daddy's girl until I wasn't,
I stopped waiting by the door for him to come home,
Then I was anyone's girl for the picking,
Searching far and wide for any man to give me a crumb of
attention,
My grandfather was already ill and lying in a hospital at
this point and I begged for him to return to health just so I
would feel that love again,
Not for the right reasons,
And so, it continued,
Along with a trail of broken hearts.

-They say the first man you love if your father...

If you are a magician,
Then I'm your assistant,
You made our love disappear,
Putting me in a crate,
Cramped and alone,
You got out your saw,
Cut through to the bone,
When the crimson appeared,
Shock lined your face,
I don't know if I will get out of this dark space

-Our love had no magic but our heartbreak does

The word "beautiful" never uttered from your chapped lips,
Hungrily you unlaced me like a prize,
A lion hunting the gazelle,
Just prey for you to catch,
Another tick off the list of life,
A notch on your bedpost,
A little wife to keep indoors,
Hidden behind her books and chores,

-Is that all I ever was for you?

Loved at your best,
Head in your hands,
Words pouring out your chest,
Lies permeate the air,
But I was still there,
I sat on my throne the queen of nothing,
An empty belly with no butterflies,
We never had that spark or twinkle in our eyes,
The castle I built us had started to crumble,
For once in my life, I began to feel humble.

-Was it over before it began?
I am still a queen in my own right.

I open up the window to a new day,
Tears still stain my red puffy face,
I've picked up the pen so many times,
Words locked in my throat,
Perish and die.

Another entry for the journal I never meant to keep,
The book I never wrote,
Drafted pages full of hope,
I lay on the floor a heap.

Outside beckons a new dawn,
Another day for me to mourn.

- I think I will take that drink now.

Where is your spark?
Where is your light?
You are a candle that's winked out during the night.

The wick burnt out,
The scent isn't right,
Wax on the carpet,
Unsightly burn marks when you turn on the light.

Where is my spark?
I put it to bed,
It's under my pillow,
Above it- my head.

I hid it away,
Kept it from you,
I was wasting my time,
And I had no clue.

- Everyone keeps asking me where my spark is gone, but I just want sparkling wine.

You've stabbed me in the heart with your gilded dagger,
You never meant too.

I didn't mean to fall for you,
All those nights we spent up late on the phone,
The tears we cried together,
I've added onto your burdens
The load you carry is so heavy,
I said I would be your knight in shining armour,
The drawbridge slowly closed,
Water in the moat lapping,
You were never a damsel in distress but someone who
needed a friend,

-And I ruined it all.

Your bags are packed,
Shoes waiting by the front door,
One day you will leave for the last time and not come here
anymore,
Crater left inside my stomach.
Heart an empty cavity,
Months passed,
I filled up the empty spaces with books and coffee,
A new pair of shoes by the door,
A man with wild eyes,
When he left,

-It somehow hurt me more.

The phone works both ways.

How long has it been now?
Excuse after excuse,
A fragmented relationship,
You became the recluse,
Our issues started early,
I felt I was the one to blame,
If the phone works both ways- then why don't you reply?

I have tallied up the missed calls and messages,
Your alibi is dry,
"Work is busy"
"I went on holiday"
I waited several days for a reply,
I guess you just don't care,
My heart was already broken,
I won't try messaging again.

-You could have written a letter

Heartache and heartbreak are a curse I wouldn't put among my worst enemy,
Losing pieces of yourself with every fragment you give away,
One day there will be nothing left in your chest but a cavernous hole,
You'll fill it with men and women you spend the night with,
But in the morning, you must return them to themselves,

-If you have left anything of them at all.

Who am I without you?
I am myself, I shall say.
I am light and free without your limitations that you placed
on me.

I have grown and changed without the cotton wool you
wrapped me in,
You shaped me like clay,
Moulded me into a smaller version of myself when there is
so much good in me,
I killed parts of myself to keep you happy,
Locked away my thoughts out of fear,
You never knew how to handle me,
I think you wished I was just a fuck,
But silly you,
All those years we spent together,
And you have nothing left to show for it.

-I am learning to grow back my spine

He doesn't see the darkness creeping,
Oblivious to my mental state,
I laugh and joke robotically,
The perfect little wife.

Dinners on the table darling,
 Be careful its piping hot,
The house is clean,
Babies bathed,
Do you think I can read a chapter of my book?

This marriage was a labour of love til it was just labour,
You couldn't keep on top of the dust on the shelves or the
cobwebs between my legs,
Everything was a chore,
You didn't want me anymore.

-At least on my own I clear up after myself

I wish you could see through my eyes how I see myself,
The darkness that slithers inside me,
A serpent of hate for myself,
He whispers to me the words I know are true,
Turn the knife to your skin and cut out all the bits you hate,
We will start with the eyes that looked at a man with love,
Then we will cut your heart that has given too much,
Lungs that can't seem to take in enough air,
Your womb that worked just the once,
Your belly that men advert their gaze from.

-Infact we will chop you into bits.

What is a daughter to me?
A daughter is my whole world,
The universe evolves around her laugh,
A gift from God if I believed in him,
Her tears shatter my world into glass,
Pure fascination masks my face from the smallest things
she says,
Every day I pray is a good day for her,
Any moment I am away, I want to be with her.

What is a daughter to him?
Months without contact, doesn't he care?
Not even an afterthought, it's like I'm not there.
No "Hi" Or "Hello" from the end of the phone,
I would be lucky to be contacted on birthday- even if I am
alone,
No invites to Christmas, not even a card,
"Life's tough babe" Believe me dad, I know it's hard.
But how would you know? You never ask?
It's like contacting me is a menial task,
So, I turn to poetry, my words like a flood,
Everyone's family to you except your blood.

What I wish a daughter was to him is someone for him to
love and care for,
A person to ask "how was your day too?" and really listen.
To praise mine and my siblings achievements when we
achieve,

To open up his arms for warm hugs that feel like home and
don't smell like cigarettes or beer,
I wish a daughter to him would be where memories are
made and fondly looked back on,
I wish a daughter to him was a gift,
Not a chore that he never wanted,
We have been swept under the carpet and forgotten.

-My daughter is my world

We stopped wearing our rings before it was over,
I noticed one day you hadn't been wearing yours,
And I stopped wearing mine,
It just felt like the time.
It didn't take long for the sun to fade the mark of where it
had once been,
The dip in my finger disappeared like my feelings,
I guess you stopped loving me before I realised it.

The rings we shopped for excitedly in our early twenties
meant nothing in the grand scheme of everything,
Mine is in the bottom of the sea, or it's drifted far away,
You still have yours, or so you have said,
But recently I was sure I found it under my side of the bed.

I hid it away, the shame if it all washing over me,
Threatening to drown me,
How could I have been so stupid to not see what was in
front of me?

The nights I spent alone wishing for you to come home,
Waiting for an ounce of your attention,
Begging for compliments that didn't feel like compliments
at all,
Buying a cat for company.

-Why wasn't I enough?

I blew out the candles, watching the remains of smoke
dance across my orange walls,
The doorbell rings out in the hallway,
You came like you said you would,
You weren't a first choice but an option of self-destruct,
A choice to forget myself for a night and become someone
else,
We don't even like each other,
It may be closer to hate but it's easy to fall back into old
habits,
What we create is raw and real,
It dulls the ache,
But now I just feel regret.

-The colour orange makes me happy now

How bitter and twisted we have become,
I cannot hear the voice I loved when words leave your
mouth,
We have grown thorns and thicker skins,
What once was love has been replaced,
I feel sick to my stomach when your name appears,
Our old life feels like an echo in these four walls.

-Time to cut back these thorns

I wonder if I have ever been in love.
Was I just a slave to my other desires?
I wanted to be perfect,
Caught in a mediocre life,
Nothing ever spoken about in detail,
"I am always here for you"
Etched into my skin,
When you weren't there at all,
Doomed to repeat my mother's mistake,
I took on an absent soul to have and to hold,
Poured from my cup to fill him up,
Until I had nothing left to give at all.

-I would still be here for you

I don't want to hate you,
But I don't love you either.
I don't know if we loved each other at all.
You were my lifeboat in a storm,
I was your maid, mother, nurse and wife.
I gave you all I had until I was scraping at the bottom of the
barrel,
The best years of my life all for you,
A child of ours that I grew in my womb,
Money, I earnt, you spent.

-We cannot be friends when all you do is take,
Friendships is not a one-way street.

I burnt our wedding photos,
It wasn't the best day of my life.

"Let's runaway and get married" I begged you,
Your mother chose my dress,
and you chose all the guests,
I wrote your vows,
and organised the event I didn't want to go to at all.
"I want to wear dungarees and eat pizza on the beach" I
said,
I wore the white gown and took off my crystal crown,
I booked the whole day,
Bought the decorations,
Booked the celebrant,
Saved for your suit,
Planned the honeymoon and packed our bags.

-I did it all for a day I didn't want.

I miss you,
I feel your words,
They touch my soul in places I didn't know existed,
In this lifetime I believe we were meant to meet even just
for a moment,
You brought out the sun in my eternal night,
You were the safety of a street lamp on my way home in
the dark,
The lamp left on in the hall,
A cup of tea in bed when the shadows creeps in.

-I miss you

Sometimes I wonder if I am too fucked up to be loved,
Am I too much of all the bad things I collected from my
life?

I carry around my baggage in a suitcase with me,
The wheels are stiff and squeak when they roll,
Inside a collection of books, each story is one I wrote,
I didn't get to choose all the chapters myself, sometimes
they were written for me,
If you read them, would you still pick me?

-I guess I am a library of misery.

I watch TV shows and movies depicting dates so differently
to my experiences,
Late night messages asking if I am awake,
Downing pints in shabby pubs asking if we can go back to
mine,
Expensive cocktails that I purchase myself,
We don't talk all night forging connection,
There is no nervous, sweet first kisses to my recollection,
It's all hands grabbing my sides and forceful disposition.
How I wish to watch the sunset, stay up laughing all night,
Or sit in a park watching the world go by,
Drink coffee while chatting about our lives,
But modern dating seems to be all daggers and cloaks.

-Fuck this

So many times,
I would have given you the air from my lungs,
Ripped my heart out of my chest,
Leave the trail of blood on the floor to remind you who is
the best.

I carved your name on my skin with a heart, like i would on
a tree,
I tattooed your name on my skin, but you still couldn't see
me,
You asked me what I fear, and I wrote you a list,
And every time you I saw you – you created a new fear for
me with your fist,
I was bloodied and broken laying hopeless on the floor,
It took another man to show me, how to walk out our front
door.

-Breathless

You were too small, but you were mine,
I wrote you a letter,
I never got to send,
No one understands pain like I do,
We didn't get to meet on the best terms when we did,
I was too young, and he was all wrong inside,
A broken relationship, broken girl from a broken home,
In this situation I felt all alone,
When I saw you on that screen my world scattered and the
stars collided,
I remember tears streaming down my face like tiny knives
that I wish I could have dug into myself,
I pictured pushing a pram at my tender age,
Scraping by,
Such a different life,
But it never happened in the end.
You were too small, but you were mine.

-Phoebe.

As the rain hammered against my window,
I fell into a black hole of my despair,
I cannot crawl back out,
Lost to the void,
Don't follow me,
I'll drag you down.

-I don't need saving, I need time.

Now I can see,
Blindfold removed,
You were a plaster over the wound,
The last twig in the dam,
I used you to find my missing parts,
Fabric fraying at the edges,
I will stitch myself back together.

- You cannot use another person to fix you

Inhale,
Exhale,
Thats all you have to do.

Keep yourself breathing,
Keep yourself fighting,
Keep yourself together,
Please.

-Do it for me, if you won't do it for you

I hate myself for dialling your number that evening,
Desperation aching between my thighs,
I called, asked and you delivered.
When you left me in those sweaty sheets,
A shiny wrapper left on the floor,
Red marks around my wrists,
I regretted it all.

A pretty man couldn't give me what I really needed,
As I rinsed the taste of him out of my mouth,
I promised myself I wouldn't call him again.

-Yes, I did call him again, yes, I did regret it

And just like that,
It was over,
Touch me, I beg,
No one will ever love me again,
I am easily discarded,
I will search all my life for a man to kiss the tears out my
eyes,
Piece me back together when I shatter so completely,
And hold me up before I collapse,
But now,
I watch my life fall down just like dominos.

-Why is this happening again?

Would you undo it all?

If we could go back to the street corner,
Under the light of the moon,
The December frost caresses our skin,
The alcohol tinges our breath,
Numbers exchanged,
We never knew years of our lives would be spent together
in that moment.
But if you could go back,
Would you undo it all?

-The night we met

I am so fucking tired,
I wash the aches and pains from my bones in a bath so hot
it could melt off my skin,
My eyes are red and bloodshot,
My stomach aches like someone has punched me in the gut,
The moon has disappeared in the sky like someone blew
out a candle,
The sky is just black.

-I hope I am not getting bad again

I feel like a slave to my darkest vices,
I see them staring back at me in the mirror,
My reflection grins a toothy smile and crooks her finger,
"You should be more like me" she whispers seductively,
I could fall into her trap, and lose my way back,
I am addicted to the attention,
Shower me with compliments,
Let me overpower you and show you what I can do.
Weeks later the guilt will come crawling in.

-Why can I not control myself?

Here he is again,
Crawling through the broken promises of our last
conversation for an evening with me,
He wants the connection without the effort,
Desperate for my touch, he doesn't want to have to ask for
it.
As he crawls through his oaths,
Just for another taste of me,
The words with suffocate him this time.

-No second chances for you.

Anxiety's hands claw at my throat,
I can't breathe,
My thoughts are out of control,
I am caught between black and white,
Acid rises,
Will you be my alkaline?

-Someone balance me out.

I just want to dance in the rain,
Swim in the sea,
Fuck in the sand,
But I am stuck Infront of the TV.
I want to laugh till I scream,
Cry till it hurts,
Run among the hills through the long grass,
But I am glued to my phone, hoping someone likes my
post.
I am stuck behind this desk, the phone relentlessly ringing,
Typing up documents, printing, cutting, pasting,
Endlessly time wasting,
I am stuck cooking, wiping, spraying, hoovering,
scrubbing, making lists, shopping, making more lists, again
and again,
Every fucking day the same thing.

-Will it ever change?

You could build him a home,
Decorate the walls,
Furnish the rooms and halls,
Make the bed up with pillows and sheets.
He will take it apart brick by brick and complain about the draft.

-It wouldn't matter if you built him a mansion, he would look for a hotel to stay in.

I didn't wake as you slid into bed next to me,
A familiar pattern over the last few years,
I was always an early riser,
You a night owl.
We became the moth and the flame,
I knew one day we would burn each other,
And never sleep next to each other again.

-I don't mind the empty bed so much anymore

I wasn't ready.
I wasn't ready for my life to flip upside down,
For my chest to ache as much as it does,
Lonely evenings on the sofa,
Music fills my ears but I don't hear the lyrics,
Cooking alone, with just myself to feed.
For an empty bed, not even a cat to curl up next too,
I wasn't ready to think about Christmas 's and Birthdays
alone,
Alternating celebrations with my daughter who I carried for
9 months,

-I wasn't ready, at all.

LUST

He licks his lips like I am a meal to devour,
I am his starter, main and dessert plated up before him on a
silver platter,
He wants to feast upon me like a starved mad man.

"You, are dangerous" he whispers into the shell of my ear.
He is the wolf and I am the rabbit,
He is predator and I am prey,

-This is not a love story.

I ride the waves you blessed me with,
You are God controlling my tide,
I am as wet as the ocean,
I sparkle in your hands,
Like a siren,
I pull you in,
Drowning you.

-Guess what this is about.

You and I could scorch the earth,
Hot, slick and sticky skin,
Sweat dripping onto cotton sheets,
Unspoken words burning into my tongue like hot coffee,
Eyes shining like dying stars in a perfectly clear night sky,
The smallest touch makes me stomach dip and my body
sway.

We are nuclear,
We are catalysts,
We have no end and no beginning.

-I need more nights like these

I am not a performer,
I am not a professional,
But you are.

You make me shudder and shiver,
I cry out your name,
I have forgotten my own.

I need more,
More of you,
More of this.

My breath hitches,
Legs quiver,
Eyes roll back,
If this is heaven, please let me stay.

-I can only imagine your body count

I saw you,
You made me feral.
A wild thing.

I gouged out the walls of my prison to get to you,
Tearing off my clothes and skin,
You had a devilish smile,
A smirk to contend with the devil,
Savage untamed beast,
Deliverer of earth-shattering pleasure.

Knee-buckling,
Sheet clutching,
Thigh clenching,
Lip biting,
Feral.

-I never want to leave this bed

Like a lamb for slaughter on the alter,
A white dress lays discarded on the floor,
Naked body for you to paw,
You never cherished my body like a lover does,
But we were never lovers,
I am a sacrifice to your cause,
Use me as you please.

-I am yours

Trace the letters of your name on my skin,
With your fingers or your tongue,
Only you and I will know it's there.
Just for tonight you will own me,
Just for tonight, I am yours.

-What's your name again?

The river flowed past us,
Sat on a wooden picnic bench,
Legs stuck together,
The summer's heat baking our skin,
Making us sin,
I sip my whisky neat,
You drink beer,
Large calloused hands grip mine.
You ask me what I'm into,
I see the twinkle in your eye,
I know you will ask if you can take me home tonight.

- Do I say yes?

I ordered a bottle of wine for the table,
The table legs wobbled like my own,
A familiar face sits across from me,
Gone was the boy you once were and now in front of me
sits a man.

Teenage dreams and in-betweens dance across my eyes,
First date with an old flame,
A passionate kiss under a half-moon,
The ocean waves crash behind us,
Cold air skims across my untouched skin,
I want you to lay me down under this grey sky and show
me what years of longing feels like.

-Looking back now, this was a terrible idea

Religion doesn't touch my soul like you do,
Pulling apart the fabric of my being like it was simply wool
on a loom,
You weave my fate into a tapestry,
Perhaps we were already doomed.

I would let you tie me down and carve out my heart just to
watch it beat,
A blade that writes your name on my thighs because
ownership and control is the ultimate goal,
I would do anything to please you.

You could drip poison between my chapped lips,
Venom from a snake coiling through my veins,
Heat burning through my body and setting me alight,
You'd make me crave for death as if it was just a holiday.

I am merely your servant,
Worshipping on bruised knees with cut palms,
Waiting to be discarded like an old bride.

-Poison couldn't kill me

If your body is a temple,
My body is a ransacked church,
The stones are crumbling down around us,
I get down on my knees to worship daily,
You stand above me towering like a god,
Praising me with your words,
Actions never taken on my prayers to you.
If I were a religious woman,
I would find a new god.

-Worship me

Spread my thighs like a knife spreads butter,
I want to lose myself in something else that isn't misery,
Lost on a road of pleasure,
My mind wanders to happier times,
Butterflies try to escape the confined space inside my belly,
My aching heart is beating so fast,
The butterflies will carry it far away,
Please just make me feel more than what I am,
More than what I know.

-I wish I were free like a butterfly

Tuesday evening,
A sunsets warmth reflects onto white walls in a half empty
room,
Two legs intertwine on a sofa that is sinking in,
Dirty fingers clasp around my throat,
Words and moans claw out my mouth,
These are not sweet nothings,
This feels like sweet something,
Heady breaths against the column of my throat,
Breathe into me a breath of life,
I see music in the air as it plays from a phone a room away,
Colourful sprites twinkle in front of my eyes,
A rainbow of colour,
If he squeezes harder then maybe I won't see Wednesday.

- You have me in a chokehold

You lit the fire in my veins,
Mossy eyes undress me slowly,
Hands trailing up and down my unperfect body,
Arms wrapped around the parts I don't like,
The light turned off so we are illuminated only by the
evening sky,
He turned on the lamp and said "Let me see all of you."
I think my heart new then,
I would have to learn to love one day,
Even if I am turned away.

-Is this love?

Your very existence sets me aflame,
Body aflame with just the thought of you,
You stoke the flames with your words and gentle caresses.

My chest aches and my heart beat's out of its prison,
A cadge unlocked and a monster set free.

Hands by my side in clenched fists, they yearn to touch
you,
Fingertips longing to feel outline your figure,
I long for your body pressed up against mine,
Quiet evenings just him and I.

-I am not alone, I am just lonely.

I am not fragile,
I am a woman,
Treat me roughly,
Hold me close,
Bend and break me then watch me rebuild.

Caress and bite me,
Whisper sweet nothings into my neck,
Kiss me hard like I were made of stone,
Push me to the precipice and be my life line.

- No man can take me over the edge these days

When was it over?

It was over when I laid down at night and imagined anyone
but you lying next to me.
When shopping lists filled my head when you took me to
bed.

In my dreams I created my man,
They said please and thank you,
Tall, dark handsome and kind.

Envisioning my wildest fantasies kept our spark alive,
A hand in cotton panties,
Panting by your side,
While I tolerated you,
I slept next to a new man every night.

- Am I a bad person? Probably

Before day breaks,
And the sunrise paints its colours across the sky,
I will watch you sleep soundly,
Your hand resting on mine,
The rise and fall of your chest a melody that calls to me,
Each breath creates a symphony,
Your profile is begging to be painted, sculpted and etched,
A masterpiece,
Has anyone told you that you look like art before?

- He looks like art in its purest form

We didn't exchange words,
Just sounds,
Animalist,
Our bodies were twisted,
You were a lighthouse and I crashed against your shores
over and over,
The light never went out,
I collided with you again and again,
When you were done with me,
You rescued me from the shore and gave me a new boat,
And then pushed me back out to sea.

- I do not regret you at all

"What inspires you?"
Lying in bed,
You twist my hair through your fingers like you could
weave it into golden thread,
Your eyes pierce through my soul,
Our shadows on the bedroom wall,
You look at me expectedly,
Wanting to hear the words I feel I cannot speak,
So instead, I just say
You.

-When is it too soon to say "I love you".

The sound of a knife hitting the chopping board,
Wine trickling into a mug and not a glass,
Sweet hums from your throat,
Your arms snake around my waist,
Hands tucked inside the back pockets of my jeans,
And squeeze.

I wonder if I will always want you as much as I do now?
Every time we go to bed the earth shatters and stars collide,
But I am starting to see you are frozen inside.

- I am moving on, but I don't think I'm moving up.

Do you remember when we sat outside on the rickety
wooden bench,
I perched on your lap,
Your hands tracing the tattoo at the top of my thigh,
The rain drops fell upon us,
Crystal clear and hard as rocks,
Our eyes closed as the water kissed our eyelids and our
giggles sounded like bells,
We pulled a woollen blanket over our heads offering soft
protection from gods wrath,
"Let's go to bed."
This was the day that I was yours, and you were mine.

- If I asked you now about that day, I think you would have
forgotten.

Rough hands hold my soft cheeks,
Like a rock caressing a rose petal,
A forehead is pressed against mine,
Salty sweat running down our faces like a river,
Laboured breathing in each other's spaces,
A volcano has erupted between us,
The heat is stifling,
I think it might kill us.

- I forgot how it felt to fall in love, and I'm scared.

I met a man who could turn wine into water,
He sipped it like a life line and it helped him keep his
promises,
Like a wishing well - he took my gold,
Fulfilling oaths all around,
A prince of lies sits at the head of the table,
Open thighs I was his feast,
He lapped at me like a starved crazed fool,
I felt like the sweetest desert,
Dripping honey onto his tongue,
Whispering lies for him to hear,
I stole his crown.

- This man has a wicked tongue.

You took the fire out my throat,
Eased the burdens that I bared,
An older man with ideas,
You didn't laugh at mine.

The marks decorating my skin do not disturb you,
You have lived a full life before me,
Taken to bed women with scars, stretch marks and faded
tattoos,
All shapes and sizes to pleasure you.

No longer am I a teenage girl rebelling against her father,
But if I take you to bed,
Then I guess I am,
Because you are an older man.

- I wish I could take it back but I can't.

Can I borrow your eyes, my love?
I just want to see how I look to you.
Do my curves look better from this angle?
Belly rolls carved in like the statue of Athena,
My lips plump like peaches,
Are my eyes like diamonds or sparkling pools of cool
water?
When I open my legs to you, do you see nirvana?

- I hope you think I am pretty.

I ache inside,
I am molten lava,
A volcano waiting to erupt,
Desperation and need clings to my soul,
Magma threatens to escape me,
I shine like polished obsidian,
Don't come to close as I threaten to erupt

-I am a ticking time bomb

I dreamt I was a contortionist in your carnival,
The lights were bright and the noise loud,
You bent me in every which way you could,
Backwards & forwards,
Upside down,
You forced me to stay,
Work every day,
The crowd begged for me,
I gave them a show,
I asked for it fast,
You told me no,
The spotlight shone on,
The clapping receded,
I could have been all you needed,
Now I'll stop performing,
The performance will dwindle,
Till you take no notice,
Find another lover to swindle

- Are you the Carnival Master?

Dusky skies illuminate a darkened hallway,
Summer heat stifles the air,
Black lace skims past my breasts like the hands of a lover,
My hair is unbound and wild,
The door opens wide revealing a face I have known for
years,
Heated glances are exchanged,
A silent communicated agreement,
Show me what you came here for?

-Here we go again.

I pull a card from your deck,
You told me not to check just yet,
Because you were the jester,
You reeled me in,
Or are you the puppet master?
I can feel the tugging of strings.
Bound around my ankles,
Strung up by my wrists,
I dropped my cards,
You saw them all,
I caught a glimpse of your roughish grin,
It's a good thing we are not playing poker.

-You would win at poker too

You are a shadow in the corner of my eye,
I think of you daily in the recess of my mind,
Your name is a prayer on my lips,
It tastes just like a slice of heaven,
Every mumbled word you speak is the finest literature,
Your tongue a sniper,
And I am the target.

-How do I feel like this?

You left a bitter taste in my mouth,
My tongue swirled round,
Savouring the moment,
Hands in my hair,
Nails digging into your calves,
Hums of appreciation cannot be denied.

Bruises kiss each of my knees,
Lacy knickers pulled to the side,
Ragged nails scraping against skin on my back,
I could make my home here just looking up at you.

-Can I taste you again?

It doesn't matter how many bodies you have laid with,
Side by side,
Holding hands,
Heads on chests,
Or opposite sides of the bed,
This is your body,
Your vessel you use,
Do not deprave yourself of pleasure because of labels,
It will all mean nothing in the end.

-Life is short

Its 9pm,
I'm changing the sheets that smell of you,
Our sweat still clings to my skin,
Your cologne is in the air,
Fingertips mark my skin the colour of lavender,
I had spat out my words to the girl in the mirror,
"Why did you do this again?"

-I thought I learnt my lesson

I am the garden of Eden,
Pluck my fruits as they call to you,
I am ripe and juicy,
I will drip from your lips down your chin,
A taste like no other,
Admire my leaves,
The roots of my trees,
Be gentle with my petals,
Let's sin together.

-You will never find another like me

You touch me and I melt like chocolate,
Dripping sugary syrup between my lips,
The sweetest taste of sin,
I will never lose the taste of you in my mouth,
You are the kindling and I am the flint,
We burn together brightly,
I am the flame that will never burn out.

-Another lifetime, another lover

I crave attention and touch,
I feel the sun kiss my skin and I wish it was a familiar pair
of lips,
When the shadows and darkness creep in, it is you
wrapping me in a blanket,
I wish I could feel arms around my waist one last time,
But you are a ghost.

-Ghosted

I have taken control of my situation,
Sexual liberation,
If I want a new body under mine every night,
Then I will take it,
I don't want to remember names,
I want to remember pleasure,
Give me the time of my life,
I don't know how long I have,
In this mindset.

-But I am too scared to trust another man with my body

Pick my petals one by one,
Mind my thorns they are sharp,
I will draw blood and won't apologise,
Scarlett splatters turn my colouring from white to pink,
Pink like the colour of blush on my cheeks when you tell
me you want me.

-I smell of roses but I taste of fire

He tasted the boiling pasta so I wouldn't have too,
Blew on the sauce,
Let me lick it off the spoon,
Placed our plates in the sink and rinsed them,
Led me by the hand to the bedroom,
Laid me down gently and peeled off my clothes,
Worshiped me on his knees but never delivered me to the
holy lands,
Told me I was pretty, never beautiful,
I couldn't touch his soul so I touched his body instead.

-Poor me

When will we cross over the boundaries of lust and cross
into love,
The holy land of promise and everlasting life,
Love is the answer to my prayers,
But lust is the promise I can keep,
Will I be accepted for the broken mess I have become?

-Religion didn't work for me

Open the door to unknown wonders,
I don't know you as well as I know myself but you have
memorised my body like a map
in three minutes.
You speak different languages against my skin with your
tongue,
You are the reward for my patience,
You took me off the earth into orbit,
I reached the stars and the warmth filled my soul,
I can't come down,
I would give you a standing ovation for this performance,
But its three minutes until the second act.

-Three minutes

You top up my glass of wine,
Crimson liquid touches my lips and coats my throat,
A devilish smile and wine-stained teeth before me,
Hands gripping hips, spilling liquid,
I have whispered my prayers,
We have broken bread and drunk the wine,
Let's take this communion to bed.

-You and I can make music

I long for nights curled up by a fire, strong around me,
Conversations that last all night and end in feather light
kisses,
Laughter that hurts your stomach and leaves you breathless.
I want a man who knows what he wants and who he is and
will wait for the night I will take him to bed,
Someone to dance with when our favourite song comes on,
And a shoulder to rest my head,
I want romance,
Rose petals across silk sheets,
Words of praise when I sink low on my knees,
Eye contact,
Something that is raw and real,

-Give me something I can **really** feel

Gaze at me like the stars in the sky,
Watch me fly across the atmosphere and wish upon me,
I can deliver your dreams and become your fantasies,
Lay me down in the fields above the blanketed night,
Make me forget my name and where I came from,
Let me hear the wind sing me a lullaby,
And the earth on my back with your hands wandering
across unseen.

-I want to be connected to nature and you

You have become my muse,
Your gentle teases and soft caresses beneath an amber
moon.

Crisp rust-coloured leaves dance in the air as we walk hand
in hand,
Bustling streets,
Bitter winds and warm coffees enjoyed together,
Chaste kisses from behind while pondering over books,
A smile that could melt the frost on frozen petals in
December,
Eyes that remind me of the earth,
Hints of blue and green that change in the light.
The summers fading and autumn knocks for us.

-This was one of my favourite days this year

You whimper words of praise and moan my name,
I am a prayer you recite over and over,
A poem you create with no words,
You are a canvas that I can paint,
The clay I can mould into shape,
I have tools at my disposal for us to use,
We can create something new,
Together.

But before the art begins it falls to pieces quickly,
The paper is wet, canvas is ripped, the clay is too dry,
What a shame we have to begin again.

-Drip paint all over me

I have never yearned for a man the way I have yearned for you,
Silent as death you appear like an apparition,
Hands in places Lucifer cannot reach,
Mouths pressed against hot skin,
Bare flesh on a cold kitchen counter,
Your chest heaving against mine,
Just gasps, moans and the hum of the fridge,
Your smile says it all.

-You, me and the kitchen

You make me depraved,
My bedroom fantasies are as unhinged as my jaw when I
bring you pleasure,
You make me want to do bad, wicked things,
Things I have read in books,
Things I have only dreamt of,
I worry that if I share this darkness with you,
It will make you think less of me,
Push me to the brink of insanity and bring me back,
But don't let me go too far.

-Or I won't come back

I want to chase the sunset with you,
Late nights singing in the car,
Hot chips sitting on eager laps,
The taste of salt on your tongue.
Orange and red hues painting us,
Every curve of our bodies illuminated by the setting sun,
We could have had our own golden hour in the back seat of
your car.

-What song will we sing?

The heat in that bedroom was stifling asphyxiating,
Damp and sweaty clothes littering the floor,
I am straddled upon you,
Whisky bottle in one hand and the other on your chest,
This could be the lowest I have ever sunk,
You told me you only like me because I paint sunsets,
Now I am riding my own waves of pleasure,
Drinking myself into oblivion,
Mimicking the beat of the music with my hips,
And I hope this is the last time between us.

-I thought I would stop making mistakes like this as an
adult

I am not a performer,
I am not a professional,
But you are.
You make me shudder and shiver,
I cry for more.
Give me more.
My breath hitches,
Legs quiver,
Eyes roll back, I am on another planet.

-I lust you

I feel high in the moonlight,
There is blood on the cupid arrow, and I have been hit.
I have always felt love through gritted teeth,
But the tenderness you show makes my jaw unclench and I
wonder if this time will be different.

You are the first droplets of rain in a drought,
The sun hitting its peak in a cloudless sky,
I don't want to let you go,
Or let us go,
I crave your scent, your smile, your laugh, your taste when
you are only a few miles away.

I tell myself it's a chemical reaction,
I can't reveal the lie,
It's a hormonal problem that's going on in my brain,
But the cold side of the bed tells me that life won't be the
same again.

-What are we?

We are made out of dead stars my love,
How many times have faces so similar kissed before,
Created out of a million love stories,
How blessed are we to meet in this moment and come together?
You are so scared of the word "love"
But you are yet to understand its meaning,
There are so many types of love,
Love doesn't mean forever, but it means right now in this moment,
Right now- I love you.

-Love and lust have a fine line

Am I the foolish one for being infatuated with you?
Scared to bare my blemished skin,
Un-nerved to profess any emotion that doesn't just fall
under lust,
Trapped in your gaze - you call me "perfection"
I crave your touch,
A burning inferno,
You wish for my words that will never come.
"Love? Who is he, I haven't heard of him."
Whispers on grape vines speak of great loves,
Heart shattering, mind-bending emotions,
Soul mates and twin flames,
Running to the airport to stop the plane,
Travelling 1000 Miles to see them again.

-Is this lust or more?

Thank you for reading my first ever book.
All your love and support has been amazing, I appreciate you.

Follow me on my socials

@JWGPoetry

Cover designed and illustrated by Izze Wren

@IzzeWren

Printed in Great Britain
by Amazon